3/16

GRAPHIC WARFARE

TET OFFENSIVE

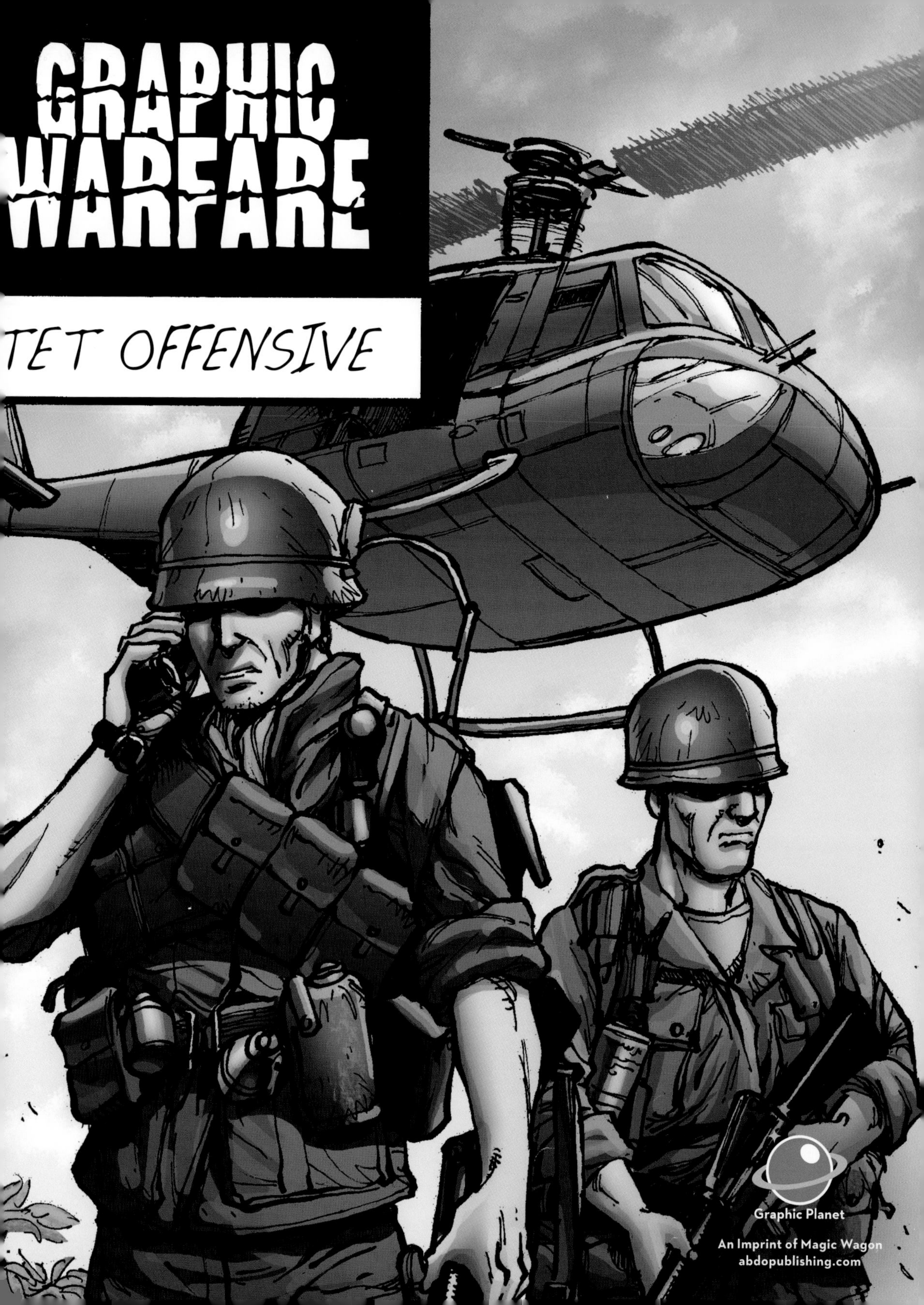

Graphic Planet
An Imprint of Magic Wagon
abdopublishing.com

ABDOPUBLISHING.COM

Published by Magic Wagon, a division of ABDO, PO Box 398166, Minneapolis, Minnesota 55439. Copyright © 2016 by Abdo Consulting Group, Inc. International copyrights reserved in all countries. No part of this book may be reproduced in any form without written permission from the publisher. Graphic Planet™ is a trademark and logo of Magic Wagon.

Printed in the United States of America, North Mankato, Minnesota.
102015
012016

Written by Joeming Dunn
Illustrated by Ben Dunn
Coloring and retouching by Robby Bevard
Lettered by Doug Dlin
Cover art by Ben Dunn
Interior layout and design by Antarctic Press
Cover design by Candice Keimig

Library of Congress Cataloging-in-Publication Data

Dunn, Joeming W.
  Tet offensive / by Joeming Dunn ; illustrated by Ben Dunn.
    pages cm. -- (Graphic warfare)
  Includes index.
  ISBN 978-1-61641-983-7
  1. Tet Offensive, 1968--Comic books, strips, etc.--Juvenile literature. 2.
Graphic novels. I. Dunn, Ben, illustrator. II. Title.
  DS557.8.T4D86 2016
  959.704'342--dc23
                    2015023940

TABLE OF CONTENTS

FOREWORD

Vietnamese civilization has existed for thousands of years. In 207 BCE, the people formed a kingdom called Nam Viet. But Nam Viet was subject to invasion by other peoples. In 111 BCE, the Chinese conquered Nam Viet. The Vietnamese people did not gain independence again until CE 939.

Different Vietnamese families fought for rule. Then, the Chinese again invaded in 1407. In 1428, the Vietnamese again regained control. But in 1858, French forces invaded Vietnam. The French gained control over Vietnam, Cambodia, and Laos, and created French Indochina.

In 1945, during World War II, the Japanese ousted the French from Vietnam. When the war ended, Vietnamese wanted independence. But France wanted its colony back. This conflict led to the First Indochina War. The Vietnamese defeated the French. The peace agreement divided the country into North Vietnam and South Vietnam.

A group called the Viet Minh took control of North Vietnam. Its leader, Ho Chi Minh, expected US support in Vietnam's bid for independence. However, Ho Chi Minh favored Communist government, which the US could not support. This began a long struggle for control of South Vietnam.

Would Vietnam be reunified? Would the North or the South gain control? Would the country's government be Communist? These questions would only be answered after more war . . .

ON JANUARY 30, 1968, THE VIETCONG AND THE NORTH VIETNAMESE ARMY LAUNCHED A COORDINATED ATTACK AGAINST THE UNITED STATES AND SOUTH VIETNAM. THIS ATTACK, CALLED THE TET OFFENSIVE, CHANGED THE COURSE OF THE VIETNAM WAR.

CHINA

Gulf of Tonkin

HAINAN

THAILAND

South China Sea

LAOS

CAMBODIA

VIETNAM

VIETNAM IS THE EASTERNMOST COUNTRY ON THE INDOCHINA PENINSULA IN SOUTHEAST ASIA. IT HAS AN AREA OF ABOUT 130,000 SQUARE MILES (336,700 SQ KM).

MOST OF VIETNAM IS COVERED WITH DENSELY FORESTED JUNGLES AND HILLS.

DURING THE LATE 1800S, THE FRENCH CONQUERED INDOCHINA. THEY HAD COLONIAL RULE OF THE REGION FOR OVER 70 YEARS.

DURING WORLD WAR II, NAZI GERMANY DEFEATED THE FRENCH IN 1940. ALL FRENCH COLONIAL TERRITORIES WERE TURNED OVER TO THE AXIS POWERS.

JAPAN WAS PART OF THE AXIS. IT SOON TOOK CONTROL OF INDOCHINA, INCLUDING VIETNAM.

WELCOM
TO
SAIG

AFTER ITS DEFEAT IN WORLD WAR II, JAPAN HAD TO GIVE UP THE TERRITORY.

IN 1945, A NATIONALIST GROUP CALLED THE VIET MINH PROCLAIMED VIETNAM'S INDEPENDENCE. ITS LEADER WAS HO CHI MINH

WE HAVE THE RIGHT TO BE FREE.

HO CHI MINH WANTED AN INDEPENDENT VIETNAM.

HOWEVER, THE FRENCH DECIDED TO RECLAIM ITS COLONIAL TERRITORIES. TO AVOID THE SPREAD OF COMMUNISM, THE US SUPPORTED FRANCE'S EFFORTS.

THE FRENCH SHOULD RETAIN INDOCHINA.

WE WILL HELP WITH TROOPS UNTIL THEY CAN MAINTAIN CONTROL.

IN JANUARY 1946, HO CHI MINH WON AN ELECTION. HE SOON DEMANDED A FREE VIETNAM WITHIN FRENCH CONTROL.

7

THE FRENCH DID NOT AGREE TO HO CHI MINH'S DEMANDS. THEY BROUGHT TROOPS INTO VIETNAM IN EARLY 1946.

THEY STARTED TO EXPEL THE VIET MINH AND ARREST THEIR LEADERS.

SOON AFTER, THE VIET MINH STARTED A GUERRILLA WAR AGAINST THE FRENCH. THIS WAS CALLED THE FIRST INDOCHINA WAR.

AT FIRST, THE VIET MINH WERE POORLY SUPPLIED. HOWEVER, THEY QUICKLY GAINED SUPPORT OF THE CHINESE COMMUNISTS.

THE CHINESE BEGAN TO PROVIDE THEM WITH WEAPONS.

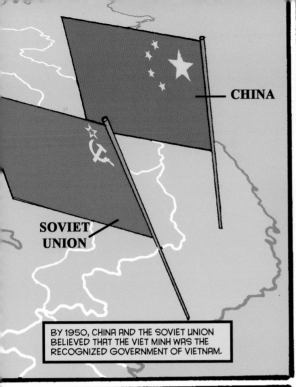

CHINA

SOVIET
UNION

BY 1950, CHINA AND THE SOVIET UNION BELIEVED THAT THE VIET MINH WAS THE RECOGNIZED GOVERNMENT OF VIETNAM.

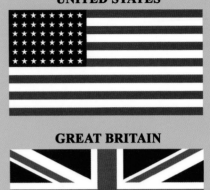

HOWEVER, THE UNITED STATES AND GREAT BRITAIN STILL SUPPORTED THE FRENCH-BACKED STATE OF VIETNAM.

UNITED STATES

GREAT BRITAIN

THIS GOVERNMENT WAS LED BY BAO DAI.

THE SOVIET UNION AND CHINA CONTINUED TO SUPPORT THE VIET MINH. PRESIDENT DWIGHT D. EISENHOWER WAS HESITANT TO INTERFERE IN THE COUNTRY, ESPECIALLY WITH TROOPS. THE KOREAN WAR WAS STILL FRESH IN AMERICAN MINDS.

I DO NOT WANT TO GET INTO ANOTHER CONFLICT.

THE FIGHT FOR VIETNAM WAS NOT GOING WELL FOR THE FRENCH. THEY WERE FINALLY DEFEATED IN THE BATTLE OF DIEN BIEN PHU IN MAY 1954. THAT JULY, THE TWO SIDES MET IN GENEVA, SWITZERLAND, TO SIGN PEACE AGREEMENTS.

THE GENEVA ACCORDS DIVIDED THE COUNTRY ALONG THE 17TH PARALLEL. COMMUNIST HO CHI MINH AND THE VIET MINH CONTROLLED THE NORTH.

CHINA

NORTH VIETNAM

LAOS

Gulf of Tonkin HAINAN

South China Sea

17th parallel

THAILAND

CAMBODIA

Gulf of Thailand

SOUTH VIETNAM

BAO DAI WENT INTO EXILE. NGO DINH DIEM TOOK CONTROL OF THE SOUTH. HE WAS OPPOSED TO COMMUNISM.

WHILE DIEM WAS FRIENDLY WITH THE UNITED STATES, HE RULED WITH AN IRON FIST.

DIEM WAS FIRMLY ANTI-COMMUNIST.

HE JAILED OR EXECUTED ANY OPPOSITION TO PROTECT HIS POLITICAL POWER.

BECAUSE OF DIEM'S ACTIONS, THE PEOPLE OF SOUTH VIETNAM STARTED TO REBEL. MANY BELIEVED THIS WAS INSTIGATED BY THE NORTH.

ON NOVEMBER 8, 1960, PRESIDENT JOHN F. KENNEDY WAS ELECTED US PRESIDENT. HE CONTINUED THE COLD WAR POLICIES OF PRESIDENTS TRUMAN AND EISENHOWER.

THE UNITED STATES WAS STILL WARY OF FURTHER COMMUNIST EXPANSION. IT HAD JUST FINISHED DEALING WITH THE CONFLICT BETWEEN NORTH AND SOUTH KOREA.

NORTH KOREA

SOUTH KOREA

AND THE BUILDING OF THE BERLIN WALL.

IT HAD ALSO FAILED IN THE BAY OF PIGS INVASION TO OVERTHROW CUBAN LEADER FIDEL CASTRO.

SO KENNEDY COMMITTED TO STOP COMMUNIST EXPANSION IN VIETNAM.

THE GUERILLA CAMPAIGN IN THE SOUTH WAS SUCCEEDING. COMMUNIST REBELS CALLED THE VIETCONG WERE ABLE TO DEFEAT THE LARGER SOUTH VIETNAMESE MILITARY.

IN 1963, A COUP BY HIS GENERALS RESULTED IN DIEM'S ARREST AND EXECUTION ON NOVEMBER 2.

THE VIETCONG AND NORTHERN VIETNAMESE TOOK ADVANTAGE OF THIS POWER VOID. THEY INCREASED THEIR SUPPORT FOR THE GUERILLAS.

DURING THIS TIME, US MILITARY ADVISERS WERE IN SOUTH VIETNAM HELPING TRAIN THE SOUTH VIETNAMESE IN THEIR FIGHT AGAINST THE GUERILLAS.

ON NOVEMBER 22, 1963, PRESIDENT JOHN F. KENNEDY WAS ASSASSINATED IN DALLAS, TEXAS.

PRESIDENT LYNDON B. JOHNSON TOOK THE OATH OF OFFICE. HE CONTINUED THE POLICY OF BATTLING COMMUNISM.

ATTACKS ON US PERSONNEL STARTED BECOMING MORE FREQUENT. HE DECIDED TO INCREASE ATTACKS ON THE VIETCONG.

THE UNITED STATES BEGAN A BOMBING CAMPAIGN. IT USED OVER A MILLION TONS OF BOMBS AND MISSILES. IT HOPED TO FORCE THE NORTH TO A CEASE-FIRE.

ATTACKS ON THE US AIR FORCE BASES FORCED THE US TO SEND IN MARINES TO HELP PROTECT THOSE BASES. THE NUMBER OF PERSONNEL INCREASED TO NEARLY 200,000 IN LATE 1965.

THE BOMBING CAMPAIGN DID NOT DISCOURAGE THE VIETCONG. THEY CONTINUED TO HAND DEFEAT AFTER DEFEAT TO THEIR SOUTH VIETNAMESE OPPONENTS.

GENERAL WILLIAM WESTMORELAND WAS THE COMMANDER OF UNITED STATES FORCES IN VIETNAM. HE DECIDED A DIFFERENT STRATEGY NEEDED TO BE USED.

HIS STRATEGY WOULD CHANGE FROM A DEFENSIVE POSITION TO A MORE AGGRESSIVE OFFENSIVE POSITION.

THE US FORCES THOUGHT THE VIETCONG GUERILLAS WERE MOSTLY POOR, UNEDUCATED VILLAGERS.

THEY WOULD BE POORLY SUPPLIED AND TRAINED.

THE US MILITARY WAS WELL SUPPLIED AND TRAINED. WESTMORELAND BELIEVED HE COULD DEFEAT THE VIETCONG AND THE NORTH VIETNAMESE WITHIN TWO YEARS.

BUT THE VIETCONG'S GUERILLA TACTICS STOPPED THE US MILITARY'S PROGRESS AS IT HAD TO THE FRENCH MANY YEARS BEFORE.

DESPITE THE VIETCONG'S SUCCESSES, MANY BELIEVED THEY WERE UNORGANIZED AND UNABLE TO MOUNT ANY TYPE OF OFFENSE.

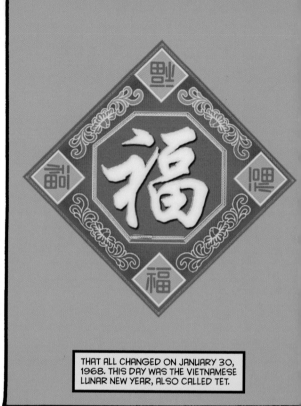

THAT ALL CHANGED ON JANUARY 30, 1968. THIS DAY WAS THE VIETNAMESE LUNAR NEW YEAR, ALSO CALLED TET.

USUALLY, THERE WAS A CEASE-FIRE DURING THIS PERIOD OF TIME.

1968

THE TEMPORARY PEACE WOULD NOT LAST LONG.

THE TET OFFENSIVE BEGAN IN THE EARLY MORNING HOURS OF JANUARY 30.

THE ATTACK COMBINED BOTH THE NORTH VIETNAMESE ARMY AND THE VIETCONG FORCES.

GENERAL VO NGUYEN GIAP WAS THE NORTH VIETNAMESE ARMY'S LEADER. HE PLANNED THE ATTACK.

HE HOPED TO INSPIRE THE VIETNAMESE PEOPLE TO REBEL AGAINST THE SOUTH VIETNAMESE AND THE UNITED STATES.

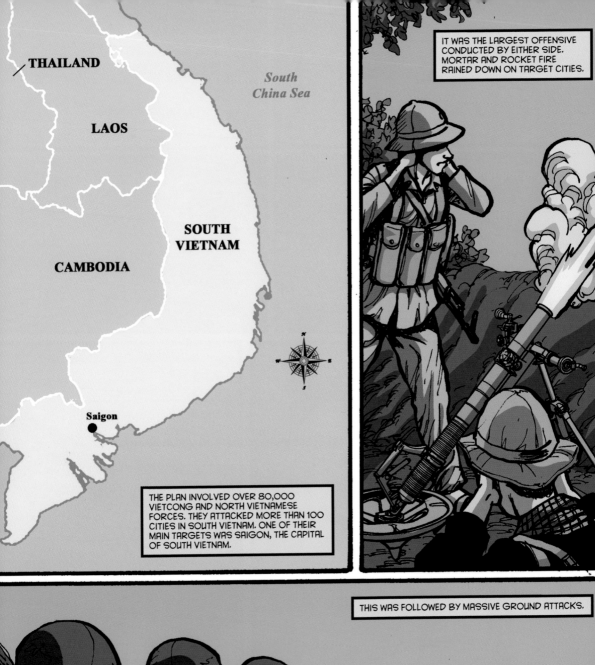

THAILAND

LAOS

South China Sea

SOUTH VIETNAM

CAMBODIA

Saigon

THE PLAN INVOLVED OVER 80,000 VIETCONG AND NORTH VIETNAMESE FORCES. THEY ATTACKED MORE THAN 100 CITIES IN SOUTH VIETNAM. ONE OF THEIR MAIN TARGETS WAS SAIGON, THE CAPITAL OF SOUTH VIETNAM.

IT WAS THE LARGEST OFFENSIVE CONDUCTED BY EITHER SIDE. MORTAR AND ROCKET FIRE RAINED DOWN ON TARGET CITIES.

THIS WAS FOLLOWED BY MASSIVE GROUND ATTACKS.

IN SAIGON, NORTH VIETNAMESE AND VIETCONG FORCES FOUND IT WAS UNREALISTIC TO TAKE THE WHOLE CITY.

INSTEAD, THEY WANTED TO CAPTURE THE US EMBASSY AND NATIONAL RADIO STATION.

NEITHER TARGET WAS TACTICALLY IMPORTANT. BUT THEY REPRESENTED STRATEGIC IMPORTANCE. THE EMBASSY REPRESENTED THE US. THE RADIO STATION WOULD BE USED TO BROADCAST A MESSAGE TO JOIN THE NORTH.

THEY FAILED TO HOLD EITHER OBJECTIVE.

19

THE ATTACK CAUGHT THE UNITED STATES AND SOUTH VIETNAMESE FORCES BY SURPRISE. BUT, THEY SOON REGROUPED.

THEY REPELLED THE ATTACKS IN MANY OF THE TARGETED CITIES AND BASES.

WITHIN A FEW DAYS, MOST OF THE GAINS OBTAINED BY THE VIETCONG AND NORTH VIETNAMESE WERE LOST.

THE VIETCONG ALSO WENT AMONG THE VARIOUS CITIES IN SMALL GROUPS. THESE GROUPS ATTACKED THE HOUSES OF SOUTH VIETNAMESE MILITARY AND POLICE OFFICERS.

THE ATTACKS WERE BRUTAL, EVEN TARGETING THE SOLDIERS' AND OFFICERS' FAMILIES.

THE BRUTALITY WAS NOT RESTRICTED TO THE NORTH.

NGUYEN VAN LEM WAS ACCUSED OF BEING A VIETCONG MEMBER AND KILLING A SOUTH VIETNAMESE OFFICER AND HIS FAMILY. NGUYEN WAS CAPTURED AND EXECUTED BY GENERAL NGUYEN NGOC LOAN. HIS EXECUTION WAS PHOTOGRAPHED BY EDDIE ADAMS AND SHOWN ACROSS THE WORLD.

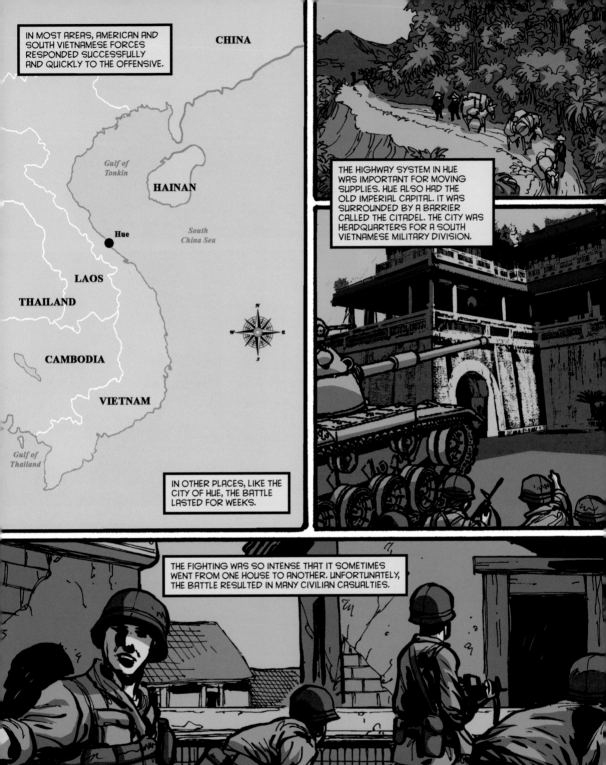

IN MOST AREAS, AMERICAN AND SOUTH VIETNAMESE FORCES RESPONDED SUCCESSFULLY AND QUICKLY TO THE OFFENSIVE.

CHINA

Gulf of Tonkin

HAINAN

Hue

South China Sea

LAOS

THAILAND

CAMBODIA

VIETNAM

Gulf of Thailand

THE HIGHWAY SYSTEM IN HUE WAS IMPORTANT FOR MOVING SUPPLIES. HUE ALSO HAD THE OLD IMPERIAL CAPITAL. IT WAS SURROUNDED BY A BARRIER CALLED THE CITADEL. THE CITY WAS HEADQUARTERS FOR A SOUTH VIETNAMESE MILITARY DIVISION.

IN OTHER PLACES, LIKE THE CITY OF HUE, THE BATTLE LASTED FOR WEEKS.

THE FIGHTING WAS SO INTENSE THAT IT SOMETIMES WENT FROM ONE HOUSE TO ANOTHER. UNFORTUNATELY, THE BATTLE RESULTED IN MANY CIVILIAN CASUALTIES.

5 CHANGING MINDS

THE TET OFFENSIVE ENDED IN MARCH 1968. NORTH VIETNAMESE AND VIETCONG LOSSES WERE ESTIMATED AT 17,000 KILLED AND 20,000 WOUNDED.

AMERICAN AND SOUTH VIETNAMESE LOSSES NUMBERED NEAR 10,000, WITH AN ADDITIONAL 35,000 WOUNDED.

MANY IN THE UNITED STATES SUPPORTED THE WAR IN THE BEGINNING. NOW THEY BEGAN TO QUESTION THE ACTIONS AND TACTICS OF GENERAL WESTMORELAND AND THE MILITARY.

DESPITE THEIR LOSSES DURING THE OFFENSIVE, THE NORTH VIETNAMESE AND VIETCONG CONTINUED TO PRESS THE ATTACK WITH OTHER MINI-OFFENSIVES.

EVEN THOUGH THE TET OFFENSIVE WAS NOT SUCCESSFUL MILITARILY, IT DID AFFECT THE ATTITUDE OF THE AMERICAN PUBLIC.

ANTIWAR PROTESTS BECAME MORE COMMON.

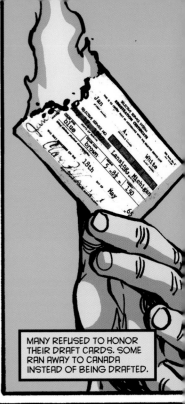

MANY REFUSED TO HONOR THEIR DRAFT CARDS. SOME RAN AWAY TO CANADA INSTEAD OF BEING DRAFTED.

OPPOSITION TO THE WAR BECAME MORE AND MORE VIOLENT. ON MAY 4, 1970, A PROTEST AT KENT STATE UNIVERSITY ENDED WITH FOUR STUDENTS BEING SHOT.

DUE TO THE INCREASING PRESSURE TO END THE CONFLICT, THE PARIS PEACE ACCORDS WERE SIGNED ON JANUARY 27TH, 1973, TO ESTABLISH PEACE IN VIETNAM.

AFTER THE PARIS PEACE ACCORDS WERE SIGNED, THE UNITED STATES BEGAN WITHDRAWING ITS TROOPS. ON APRIL 29, 1975, THE LAST US PERSONNEL LEFT SAIGON.

THE FOLLOWING DAY, SAIGON FELL TO THE NORTH VIETNAMESE.

BY THE END OF THE WAR, OVER 58,000 AMERICAN SOLDIERS HAD BEEN KILLED. MANY MORE WERE WOUNDED AND DISABLED. BECAUSE OF THE TET OFFENSIVE, MANY BELIEVED THE WAR IN VIETNAM COULD NOT BE WON.

DESPITE ITS MILITARY POWER, THE UNITED STATES WAS BADLY PREPARED FOR THIS TYPE OF WAR. HOWEVER, WE WILL NOT FORGET THOSE WHO SACRIFICED THEIR LIVES IN VIETNAM.

MAP

KAZAKHSTAN
MONGOLIA
KYRGYZSTAN
UZBEKISTAN
TAJIKISTAN
AFGHANISTAN
PAKISTAN
CHINA
NORTH KOREA
JAPAN
SOUTH KOREA
BHUTAN
NEPAL
INDIA
BANGLADESH
BURMA
LAOS
R.O.C. (TAIWAN)
Pacific Ocean
THAILAND
VIETNAM
PHILIPPINES
CAMBODIA
SRI LANKA
MALAYSIA
MALDIVES
INDONESIA
Indian Ocean

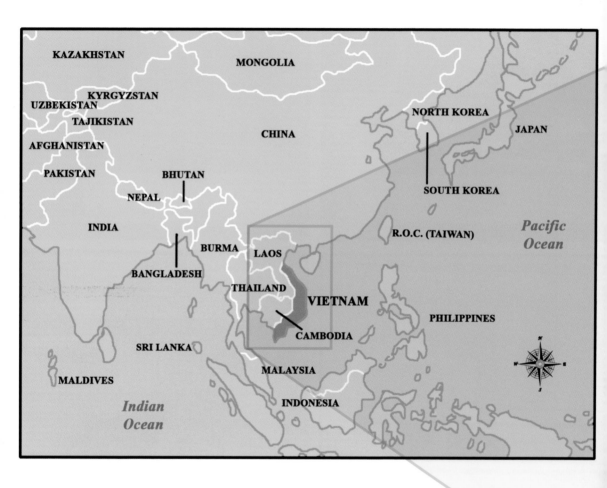

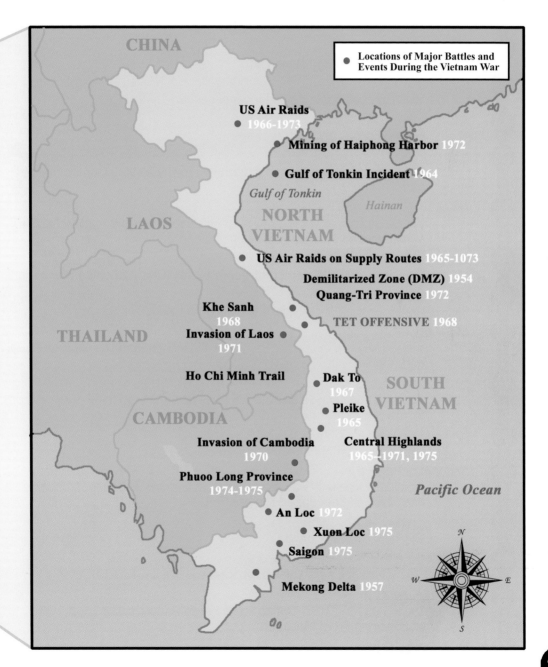

Locations of Major Battles and
Events During the Vietnam War

CHINA

US Air Raids
1966-1973

Mining of Haiphong Harbor 1972

Gulf of Tonkin Incident 1964

Gulf of Tonkin

Hainan

NORTH
VIETNAM

LAOS

US Air Raids on Supply Routes 1965-1073

Demilitarized Zone (DMZ) 1954

Quang-Tri Province 1972

Khe Sanh
1968

TET OFFENSIVE 1968

THAILAND

Invasion of Laos
1971

Ho Chi Minh Trail

Dak To
1967

SOUTH
VIETNAM

Pleike
1965

CAMBODIA

Invasion of Cambodia
1970

Central Highlands
1965–1971, 1975

Phuoo Long Province
1974-1975

Pacific Ocean

An Loc 1972

Xuon Loc 1975

Saigon 1975

Mekong Delta 1957

N
W   E
S

TIMELINE

207 BCE
The kingdom of Nam Viet was formed.

111 BCE
Chinese conquered Nam Viet.

CE 939
Vietnamese people gained independence.

1858
French forces invaded Vietnam.

1887
The French formed French Indochina from Vietnam, Cambodia, and Laos.

1945
Japanese forces took control of Vietnam from the French; Ho Chi Minh declared Vietnamese independence.

1946
French retook Vietnam; on December 19, First Indochina War began.

1950
American military advisers arrived in Vietnam.

1954 May 7
Vietnamese defeated the French at Dien Bien Phu; the Geneva Accords were signed.

1960 November 8
John F. Kennedy was elected US president; he increased support for South Vietnam.

1963 November 2
Ngo Dinh Diem was executed.

1963 November 22
President Kennedy was assassinated; Lyndon B. Johnson became president and escalated the conflict.

1968 January 30
The Tet Offensive began.

1970 May 4
Four students were killed in protests at Kent State University.

1973 January 27
The US and Vietnam signed Paris Peace Accords; the US began withdrawing from Vietnam.

1975 April 29
The last US personnel left Saigon.

BIOGRAPHIES

WILLIAM WESTMORELAND
(March 26, 1914–July 18, 2005)

General William Westmoreland commanded the US forces during the Vietnam War from 1964 to 1968. Westmoreland graduated from the United States Military Academy at West Point in 1936. During World War II, he commanded artillery forces in several theaters of operation. During the Korean War, he led a paratroop regiment and became a brigadier general. In 1964, he was named commander of US forces in Vietnam. In 1965, he became a four-star general. The Vietnamese attacks during the lunar New Year celebration of Tet on January 31, 1968, caused the American public to question Westmoreland's strategy. Later that year, President Lyndon B. Johnson called Westmoreland back to the United States. Westmoreland served as the army's chief of staff until 1972. He died in Charleston, South Carolina, on July 18, 2005.

VO NGUYEN GIAP
(August 25, 1911–October 4, 2013)

General Vo Nguyen Giap was commander-in-chief of Vietnam's armed forces. Giap joined the Communist party in 1931 and in 1939 allied with Ho Chi Minh to push for Vietnam's independence from France. In 1945, Giap declared Vietnam's independence. By 1954, French colonial rule had ended and the country was divided into North and South Vietnam. Giap directed North Vietnam's forces in the Vietnam War. He planned the attacks on January 31, 1968, during the lunar New Year celebration of Tet that became known as the Tet Offensive. In 1975, North Vietnam won the war and the country was united under Communist rule. Giap served as Vietnam's deputy prime minister from 1976 until 1982. He died on October 4, 2013, in Hanoi. He was 102 years old.

QUICK STATS

Vietnam War

Dates: 1954-1975

Number of Casualties:

United States: 58,220

South Vietnam: Approximately 250,000

Estimated for North Vietnam: Approximately 1 million

Belligerents:

The United States

The Republic of Vietnam (South Vietnam), The Democratic Republic of Vietnam (North Vietnam)

Important Leaders:

US presidents John F. Kennedy and Lyndon B. Johnson, US general William Westmoreland

North Vietnamese leader Ho Chi Minh, North Vietnamese general Vo Nguyen Giap, South Vietnamese leaders Bao Dai and Ngo Dinh Diem

GLOSSARY

accord
a formal agreement.

Axis powers
countries that fought together during World War II. Germany, Italy, and Japan were called the Axis powers.

campaign
a series of activities designed to produce a particular result.

cease-fire
a temporary stopping of hostile activities.

Communism
a social and economic system in which everything is owned by the government and given to the people as needed. A person who believes in Communism is called a Communist.

draft
to select for required military service.

embassy
the residence and offices of an ambassador in a foreign country.

expel
to force out.

guerilla
a member of a band of fighters. Guerrillas are not usually part of a regular army. They fight their enemies with sudden and surprise attacks. This type of fighting is called guerrilla warfare.

Indochina
Asia's southeast peninsula.

nationalist
a member of a political party or group supporting national independence or strong national government.

parallel
any of the imaginary lines around Earth that mark degrees of latitude.

peninsula
land that sticks out into water and is connected to a larger landmass.

strategy
the planning of military operations.

tactic
a method or a device used to achieve a goal.

Vietcong
South Vietnamese guerillas who supported North Vietnam in the Vietnamese War.

WEBSITES

To learn more about Graphic Warfare, visit booklinks.abdopublishing.com. These links are routinely monitored and updated to provide the most current

INDEX